Angel Party

Created & Written by MISTY TAGGART
Illustrated by KAREN BELL

WORD PUBLISHING
Dallas·London·Vancouver·Melbourne

Behind the third cloud to the right,
just around the corner from the rainbow, is the Angel Academy.
This is where young angels learn to be real guardian angels.

Text © 1995 by Susan Misty Taggart. Illustrations © 1995 by Karen Bell.

Trademark application has been filed on the following: The Angel Academy ™, StarCentral™,
Angel Heaven™, Jubilate™, Mirth™, Angelus™, Stella the Starduster™, Astrid™, Staria™, Miss Celestial™, Puffaluff™.

Managing Editor: Laura Minchew   *Project Editor:* Beverly Phillips

Library of Congress Cataloging-in-Publication Data

Taggart, Misty, 1940–
  Angel party/created and written by Misty Taggart;
illustrated by Karen Bell.
     p.   cm. (The angel academy; #4)
  "Word kids!"
     Summary: A young girl worries that she will not be invited to a birthday party because her grandparents' yard is full of
junk, but with the help of two angels-in-training, the party comes to her.
     ISBN 0-8499-5083-X
     [1. Guardian angels—Fiction. 2. Angels—Fiction. 3. Self-acceptance—Fiction.] I. Bell, Karen, 1949– ill. II. Title III. Series:
Taggart, Misty, 1940– Angel academy; #4.
PZ7.T1284Ar 1995
[E]—dc20
94-45102

174580

                                                                              CIP
                                                                              AC

Printed in the United States of America   95 96 97 98 99 00 LBM 9 8 7 6 5 4 3 2 1

STARIA

*She thinks she's very
grown-up, but don't
you believe it.*

ASTRID

*Her laugh is as big as
her sweet tooth.*

JUBILATE

*He's ready to right every
wrong—and has a lot
of fun doing it.*

ANGELUS

*If you have a question
about anything, he has the
answer—he thinks.*

MIRTH

*She may be small, but she
can be big trouble.*

The Angel Academy bell rang just as Staria floated happily into the room.

"Look, everyone!" she said, hugging a large, white envelope trimmed in gold. "I've been invited to the Angel Tea Party!"

Astrid couldn't believe it. Being invited to the Angel Tea Party was a very special honor. Astrid was sure the Halo and Wing Society never invited angels-in-training. "They just couldn't have invited you, Staria."

"Well, they did," Staria said.

"My invitation will be here any minute," said Mirth hopefully. She wanted to go, too.

"Special Deliverrrrry!" called Jedediah. The Operator of StarCentral was in a big hurry. He came flying through the classroom window on his bicycle! And in his hand was a big envelope.

"It's my invitation to the tea party!" Mirth called happily. Puffaluff grabbed the envelope. But it wasn't an invitation for Mirth at all. It was an Earth Assignment.

"Mirth, you're not the only one who wants to be invited to a party," said Miss Celestial.

On Earth, nine-year-old Cassie Pettigrew waited for her grandfather outside Oakbrook Elementary School. Like Mirth, she too was hoping and wishing for a certain invitation. Cassie wanted to go to Kim Miller's birthday party. But Kim and her friends never included Cassie in their plans.

Just then Cassie's grandfather drove up. *BEEP! BEEP!* He honked the horn.

Kim and her friends were standing nearby. They started whispering and giggling. Cassie was embarrassed. As usual, her grandfather's old pickup truck was piled high with junk. He was the best handyman in town.

"Why do you collect all this junk, Grandpa?" Cassie asked grumpily.

"It's not junk! All these things have possibilities. With a little special care, why you never know what they could become," he said with a smile.

He was especially proud of an old broken-down popcorn machine he had just picked up at the theatre.

At the Angel Academy, George the Heavenly Handyman had come to repair Miss Celestial's chair. He remarked, "I sure do hope Cassie gets an invitation to that party."

"What about my invitation?" Mirth pouted.

"What's so important about a party invitation, anyway?" Jubilate asked, as he tossed his sky disk.

"Yeah, who cares?" Angelus added.

Miss Celestial smiled. "I'm hoping you'll find out when you and Jubilate go on this Earth Assignment."

Back on Earth, Cassie's grandmother and grandfather just couldn't seem to cheer her up. Cassie wanted to go to that party more than anything in the whole world.

Cassie went outside to sit under her favorite elm tree. Suddenly, she heard shrieks of laughter! Then she saw two, old tires rolling down the hill toward her.

"Hey!" She jumped out of the way, just in time. The two tires tipped over and Jubilate and Angelus fell out!

"That was fun!" laughed Angelus.

Cassie couldn't believe her eyes. "Who . . . who . . . are you?"

Wings? Halos? Angel Heaven and Earth Assignments? Cassie was full of questions about her two guardian angels-in-training.

And no one else could see or hear them! Cassie loved that part. "Angelus, I've got a history test tomorrow. If you help me, no one will know."

"Study this and you won't need me!" Angelus laughed as he tossed Cassie her history book.

At breakfast the next morning, Cassie's grandfather smiled. "It's great to see you so happy."

"It must be my new friends," said Cassie.

Just then, her grandfather reached for the last jelly donut. *But, it was gone!* "Now, where did that donut go?" he asked.

Cassie giggled. She knew Jubilate had taken the missing donut.

Later in the school cafeteria, Cassie and her angels saw Kim and her friends sitting at a nearby table. Of course, none of the other children could see or hear Cassie's angels.

"Why do you want to go to Kim's party, if she doesn't want to invite you?" Jubilate asked.

"If I could go, then I'm sure we'd be friends." Cassie was about to cry. Jubilate and Angelus wanted to help.

"Come on, Jubilate!" Angelus said. The angels flew to Kim's table. And *SWOOSH!* They knocked Kim's books to the floor. A surprised Cassie ran to help Kim pick them up.

Angelus whispered, "Go ahead, Cassie, say something."

Cassie swallowed hard, "Uh . . . I guess you're excited about your . . . party."

"Oh, Cassie, I've wanted to ask . . ." But before Kim could finish, Aimee called to her, and Kim quickly ran back to the table—without inviting Cassie to the party.

The next day, Cassie was still feeling sorry for herself. "I hate being me!" she blurted out. "I wasn't invited to the party because I don't have a big house and our yard's full of junk!"

"It's not junk!" said Angelus. "Just use a little imagination. It's all got possibilities!" The guardian angel-in-training had a plan.

Back in Angel Heaven, Staria had just arrived at the Wing and Halo Society Tea Party. She politely smiled at a rather persnickety Society Angel and said, "This is a very lovely party. Thank you for inviting me."

"You're welcome, dear. But, mind your manners," the angel added, ". . . or you won't be invited back."

Of course, Staria would be a perfect little angel!

Staria chose some heavenly goodies and a cup of twinkling, pink punch. Carefully she walked toward her table. She didn't want to spill a drop.

Suddenly, Staria heard two familiar giggles. It was Astrid and Mirth peeking over a bush. Staria looked in their direction for just an instant. But that was all it took.

"Look out!" Astrid gasped. Mirth couldn't watch.

What happened next was something Angel Heaven would never forget.

The angel-in-training accidentally stumbled into a Society Angel who was also juggling her punch and plate of goodies. The Society Angel went spinning!

Bumping into one angel *might not* have been so bad. It might even have been overlooked. But . . . when that angel bumped into another angel, who bumped into another angel . . . and so on, . . . well, that was something quite different.

On Earth, Cassie was having so much fun
with her guardian angels-in-training that she
had *almost* forgotten about Kim's party.

Right there in her grandpa's yard something
incredible was happening. Jubilate and Angelus
were turning the "junk" into a playground
wonderland! She couldn't believe her eyes!

Now Cassie didn't want to be someone else.
Being Cassie was just fine with her.

On a nearby road, old Mr. Whistle's little, red bus thumped and bumped along. He was driving Kim's whole birthday party to the country for a picnic.

HAPPY BIRTHDAY KIM

Then suddenly . . . *PSSSSSTTT!* Mr. Whistle shook his head, "Sounds like we've got a flat tire!"

"Oh, no! My party's ruined," cried Kim.

But Mr. Whistle's chubby face filled with a big smile. "Maybe not. Take a look over there!" He pointed to a yard just beyond the fence.

The children cheered! "Look! It's Cassie's house!" called Kim.

Cassie couldn't believe it. Kim's party had come to her. Jubilate scratched his head, a bit confused. "I guess we're better angels than we thought."

"This is the best birthday party ever!" Kim exclaimed.

Cassie's yard was full of the most incredible rides and playthings. All of them were made from the "junk" Cassie's grandfather had collected.

Cassie's grandfather and grandmother were just as surprised at what had appeared in their yard. But Cassie was happy and that was all that really mattered.

Angelus and Jubilate thought Mr. Whistle looked a lot like George the Heavenly Handyman, but they were having too much fun to think about it.

Although the angels-in-training have never been able to prove it, the rumor around Angel Heaven is that guardian angels, like George the Heavenly Handyman and Stella the Starduster, watch over the young angels. Perhaps they even go to Earth to help them out now and again.

But, of course, Jubilate and Angelus would never need that kind of help—now would they?

Cassie's grandfather had repaired the old popcorn machine. When Mr. Whistle heard it going *POPPITY POP POP!* he was the first one in line for a box of hot, buttery popcorn.

Kim and Cassie shared a box of popcorn. "Oh, Cassie, I wish I had gotten to know you sooner. You're great!"

Cassie smiled. "Happy birthday, Kim."

"Looks like those two are going to be good friends," said Angelus, as he and Jubilate headed back to Angel Heaven.

Jubilate and Angelus beamed and their wings fluttered when Miss Celestial smiled. "You helped Cassie feel proud of who she is. And we're all very proud of you."

Then Jubilate turned to Staria. "How was that dumb old Tea Party you went to?"

Astrid giggled.
"Staria was a SMASH HIT!"
"Sounds really boring to me," Angelus added.
Then, Staria joined in the laughter.
"Not at all!" she said. "It was a PILE of fun!"

Look for these and other ANGEL ACADEMY™ books and products

at your favorite bookstore, gift shop, and retailer:

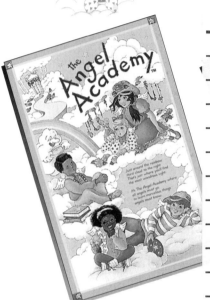

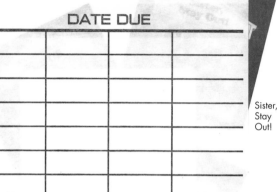

Sister,
Stay
Out!

...erry

The Angel Academy:
A Collection of Modern
Angel Tales

Don't miss the fun! KIDS CLUB.

A one-year membership inclu... ...ngel Heaven. You'll get a
Club Membership I.D. Card, ...ughout the year, and a
...urprise!

...embership, send the
...ration form along with a
...order for $10.00, per child,
...la) to:

ACADEMY™ KIDS CLUB
...480
...Dept.
...85069–9480

Do not tear out this page from your bo...
a clean sheet of paper and PRI...
_____

Child's Name: _____

Address: _____

City: _____

Phone: (_____) _____ Ag...

...for delivery. Subject to change
...ents add sales tax.

GAYLORD   PRINTED IN U.S.A.

The Angel Academy Kids Club is a division of Estee Productions, Inc.